Maybe a Glitter Soda would get his day back on track!

HOLY HOOVES!

SODA SHACK

The line was long, but Kevin was sure it would move quickly.

SMILE

It didn't, though.
And by the time he got to the front, they were out of Glitter Soda!

KEEP IT HAPPY,

he reminded himself.

SOLD OUT

SODA SHACK

Hey, friend! Don't worry! I'm gonna set you up with a free . . .

NO SMILE
NO SERVICE

KEEP IT SPARKLY WITH: GLITTER SODA

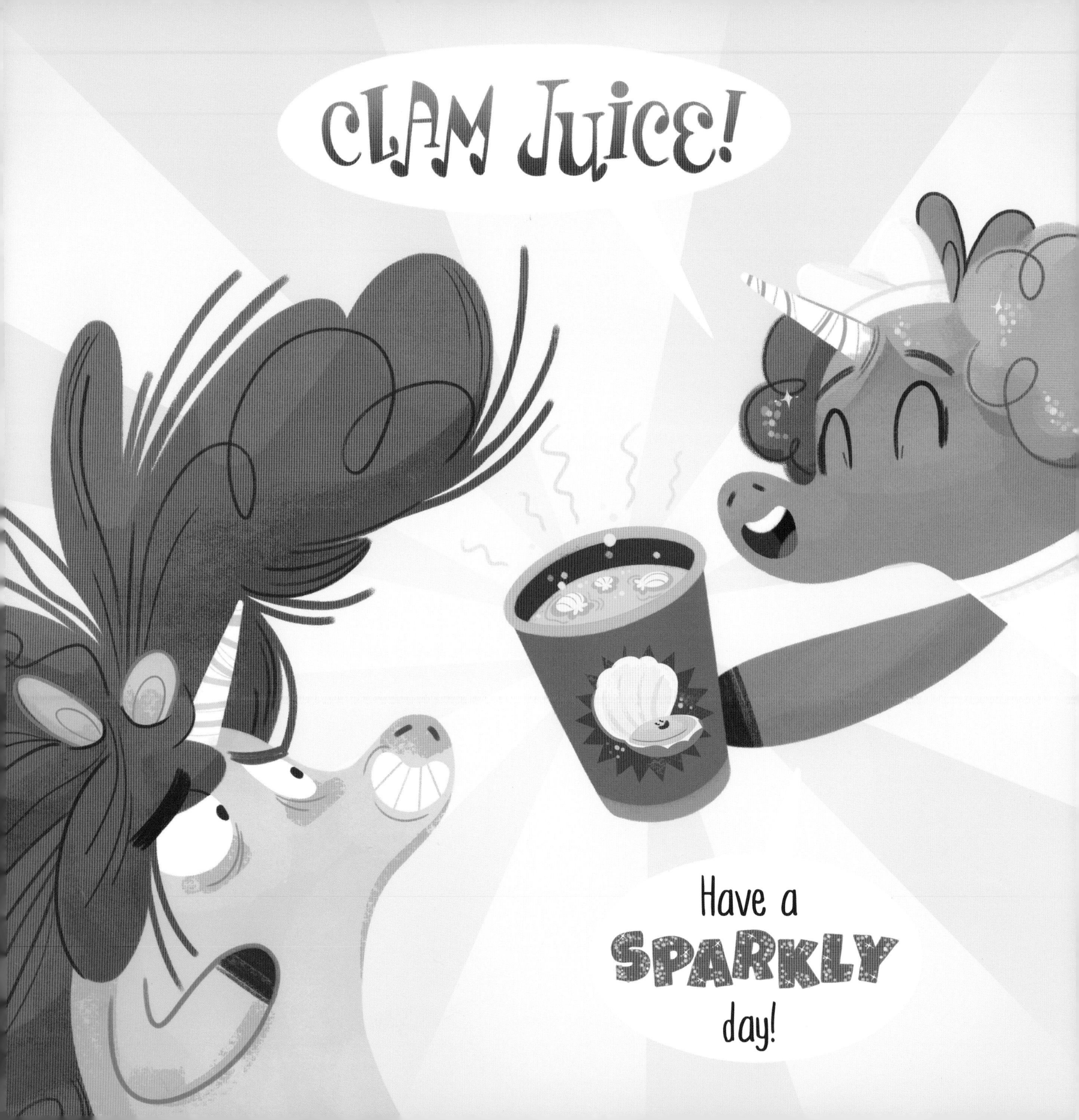
CLAM JUICE!
Have a SPARKLY day!

Kevin kept a smile on his face
even though his insides
didn't feel smiley at all.

Kevin could no longer hide what he was really feeling.

... There's clam juice on my favourite shirt.
SMILE
This has been stuck on my horn for a week and I've been pretending it's not there.

There's glitter in my eye.

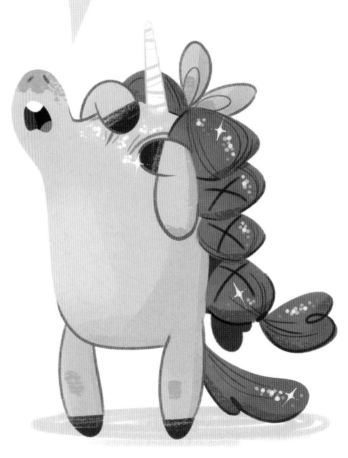

There's glitter in BOTH my eyes!

It turns out unicorns don't always have perfect, magical days.